CRANBERRY AUTUMN

WENDE and HARRY DEVLIN

Four Winds Press ❄ New York

Maxwell Macmillan Canada   Toronto
Maxwell Macmillan International
New York   Oxford   Singapore   Sydney

Four Winds Press
Macmillan Publishing Company
866 Third Avenue
New York, NY 10022
Maxwell Macmillan Canada, Inc.
1200 Eglinton Avenue East
Suite 200
Don Mills, Ontario M3C 3N1
Macmillan Publishing Company is part of the
Maxwell Communication Group of Companies.
First edition
Printed and bound in the United States of America

10 9 8 7 6 5 4 3 2 1

The text of this book is set in Baskerville.
The illustrations are rendered in watercolor and ink.

Library of Congress Cataloging-in-Publication Data
Devlin, Wende.
Cranberry autumn / Wende and Harry Devlin. — 1st ed.
p.   cm.
Summary: When Grandmother and Maggie help organize an antique sale
in Cranberryport, Mr. Whiskers feels useless until he helps
Grandmother make a big profit.
ISBN 0-02-729936-8
[1. Rummage sales—Fiction.] I. Devlin, Harry. II. Title.
PZ7.D49875Cm 1993
[E]—dc20 92-23237

For Lindsey Ann Devlin

The maple trees were turning yellow. A salt breeze came in from the sea. Summer had ended in Cranberryport, and soon the schools would open.

"School again! And we have no money for new school clothes," said Grandmother to Maggie.

"And you need a new winter coat," said Maggie. Grandmother thought about friends who needed extra money before winter set in.

Maybe it was time for the whole town to have a big sale. Everyone had old things in the attic—dolls or toys or furniture. Old things become scarce. They become antiques.

With Grandmother's help and spirit, the Cranberryport Antique Sale began to take form. Aunt Hester on the next farm had a set of blue dishes to sell. Seth from the General Store found an ancient high chair.

A breathless Mr. Whiskers, their neighbor, hauled over
his treasures for Grandmother to see.

A stuffed swordfish without a sword
A lobster-claw lamp
His second-best bathing suit
A fruitcake left over from Christmas

Grandmother held her head.
"Mr. Whiskers! Haven't you any sense at all? Get rid of
that rubbish!" she cried.

Mr. Whiskers carried it all home in a cloud of gloom. Suffering codfish! Couldn't he ever please Grandmother?

Grandmother and Maggie began to look through their attic.

They searched through trunks and boxes, closets and drawers.

Suddenly, Grandmother uncovered something rare and special—a pair of painted china dogs—wrapped in a silk shawl.

"Staffordshire dogs!" cried Grandmother. "Made in England over one hundred years ago. A prize, Maggie!" They carefully carried the dogs down to the kitchen to prepare for the sale.

News of Grandmother's sale spread to other towns, and large crowds were expected for the day.

The antique sale opened, and Mr. Whiskers still hadn't found anything to sell. He stood at Grandmother's table of antiques and sulked. No one needed him.

Mr. Grape, Mr. Whiskers's mean neighbor, stopped by Grandmother's table. He couldn't take his eyes from those beautiful Staffordshire dogs.

"Two hundred dollars," he read on the price tag. If he could get rid of Grandmother, he could outwit that foolish Mr. Whiskers, and those dogs would be his for a small price. He rubbed his hands.

Oh, how he loved to trick Mr. Whiskers.

Mr. Grape tugged on Mr. Whiskers's sleeve with a message that Grandmother was wanted on the phone.

"Oh, dear!" said Grandmother. "Mr. Whiskers, will you please take care of my table?"

"Me?" cried Mr. Whiskers. "Suffering codfish! What if someone wants to buy something?"

"Price tags are on everything," Grandmother called back to him.

While Mr. Whiskers turned to sell a silver thimble, mean
Mr. Grape cackled and removed the price tag on the dogs.

"I'll take these," he said as he handed the dogs to Mr. Whiskers. "No price tag on them, but they were twenty dollars this morning."

"Suffering codfish!" Mr. Whiskers bumbled about. What to do? Trouble already—no price tag?

A lady in an orange coat pushed in.

"Wait! Twenty dollars? Why, I'll give you two hundred!"

"Three hundred!" offered a man in a tweed jacket.

A crowd began to gather.

Up and up went the price.

Mr. Whiskers wheeled from one bid to another in baffled surprise.

Six hundred dollars! At the end of the bidding, Mr. Whiskers had sold Grandmother's dogs for six hundred dollars!

Mr. Grape stooped down and disappeared into the crowd. Grandmother returned and heard Mr. Whiskers's news.

"How wonderful! Why, you are just too smart for that mean Mr. Grape," said Grandmother. "What would we do without you?" She clapped her hands.

"I'm a hero—" Mr. Whiskers announced to Maggie. "A hero."

Later, at Grandmother's house, they celebrated with dinner.

Maggie would have new school clothes, Grandmother a coat.

"And we are going to share with friends," said Maggie.

"A new coat for you," Grandmother announced to Mr. Whiskers.

"Me? Suffering codfish! Never! This was my grandfather's." Mr. Whiskers shook his coat. A gold button fell off, and two winged creatures flew out.

"Were those your grandfather's moths, too?" Grandmother asked. Mr. Whiskers hugged his coat tight around himself and stepped outside.

"You are a wonder," Grandmother called after him.

Well, Mr. Whiskers couldn't help but agree. He smiled through his whiskers and headed home over the dunes to his little gray house by the sea. . . . Just another day of triumph for the old sea captain.

Cranberry Squares
(Ask Mother or Father to help)

1 can of whole cranberry sauce (16 oz.)
1 cup rolled oats
1/2 cup flour
1/2 cup butter
1 cup brown sugar
3/4 cup walnuts (optional)

Heat oven to 350°. Combine oats, flour, brown sugar, and walnuts. Cut butter in small pieces and combine with dry ingredients. Cover an 8-by-8-inch buttered baking pan with one-half the mixture. Cover this with cranberry sauce. Top cranberries with the rest of the mixture. Bake 45 minutes and serve warm with whipped cream or vanilla ice cream.